UNBARBAAD
FOR THOSE WHO FEEL LOST...

BY
SHOBHIT NIRWAN

© Author

First Published 2023

All rights reserved. No part of this book may be reproduced, stored in a retrieval system or transmitted in any form or by any means—electronic, mechanical, photocopying, recording or otherwise—without the prior permission of the author(s) and the publisher.

ISBN: 9789367478431
Price: ₹ 249/-

Published by

SHOBHIT NIRWAN

Printed at Tara Art Printers, Sector-5, Noida

Acknowledgements

Even a 1000 videos fall short,
To express the depth of love and support I've sought.
From Mummy, Papa, and Nimit, my dear brother,
Guiding lights, unwavering, like no other.
Their belief in me, a driving force,
Their unconditional love is a lifelong course.
Through joys and challenges, they've been my stay,
Grateful for their presence, every step of the way.

CONTENTS

❖ *Prologue*	**11 - 19**
❖ Chapter 1: (1st, 2nd, 3rd, ..., 10th} v/s 11th	**21 - 25**
❖ Chapter 2: Shah Rukh Khan: TCS Sir	**27 - 33**
❖ Chapter 3: Raksha Bandhan	**35 - 43**
❖ Chapter 4: Zeel Patel	**45 - 50**
❖ Chapter 5: Khuli Window	**51 - 59**
❖ Chapter 6: Ghar ki Murgi	**61 - 65**
❖ Chapter 7: Bahar Ke Dogale	**67 - 69**
❖ Chapters Over - Hall Started	**71 - 72**
♦ Hall - A: Tests	**73 - 82**
♦ Hall - B: Neend	**83 - 88**
♦ Hall - C: Stream Selection	**89 - 95**
♦ Hall - D: Relationships	**97 - 100**
♦ Hall - E: Physical and Mental Health	**101 - 105**
♦ Hall - F: 21 Days Challenge Scam	**107 - 109**
♦ Hall - G: Busting Out Some Weirdly Common Myths	**111 - 114**
❖ Epilogue	**115 - 115**
❖ About The Team	**117 - 117**
❖ Ruko Zara, Sabar Karo!	**119 - 120**

This book is dedicated to
YOU ♡

Prologue

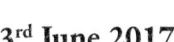

3rd June 2017

"Papa ab check karo na?...

... Abhi bhi website crash padi hai kya?" I asked my dad on call, my anxiety touching the moon.

"Ek to 2 mahine baad ye log result dete hai, aur fir yeh sab drama...

Ruko IIT Bombay jaate hi sabse pehle inki website theek karunga."

Hmm, you got it right. It was that time of the year :

The day my so-called relatives I never knew of were gonna call.

The day that had me paralyzed with stress for a week despite knowing I had done well.

Yes, my 10th boards' results day!

But, nobody in my Kota's hostel had smartphones to check their results online.

So everyone was busy calling their families ... on their *button-wala* phone.

10...

10:30...

11...

11:30...

Clock turned 12 ... and I just couldn't control it anymore!

"Bhaad mein jaaye result. Pehle pet puja karte hai," me and my two floor-mates raced to the mess.

I was about to take my plate when someone screamed from behind.

And it wasn't a usual one – the one you hear when someone is being murdered – but with an essence of joy in it.

We had already figured out the reason behind that scream before the kid mouthed a few extra words,

"Wohooooo, 10 CGPA!!!", and another, *"Tumhare bhai ki 10 CGPA aa gyi londo!,"* and another, *"10 CGPA guys, mummy mithai bhej rahi hai."*

15 minutes had passed and almost everyone received a call of appreciation from their parents except the unlucky me.

Some had come out as class toppers, some school toppers, and even district toppers too.

It seemed less like we were in a hostel mess and more like a kitty party arranged just for the top achievers of the country.

Lmaoo...

I was drooling with hunger and sweating with stress.

"Why didn't my parents call me?" I questioned my existence, "Did they abandon me already? Have I scored so low?"

5 minutes later *my dhoom-machale phone rang.*

"Haa papa jaldiiiiiii btaoooooo," my voice crackled...

"Phone par hi baitha tha kya," papa smiled.

"Arey papa batao na ..."

"Tu hi bata kya aayega? Mere bete ne vapas top kar diya aur kya! Puri 10 CGPA aayi hai mere raja beta ki. Le, mummy se baat kar le,"

"Bahut badhiya beta," said mummy, sweeping her watery eyes, all proud and happy.

"Mata rani apni kripa tujhpe hamesha banaye rakhe. Pata hai sab bol rahe hai ki ab toh bete ki IIT Bombay CS pakki samjho."

I put my phone aside and danced like 8-10 girls had said yes to marriage.

Even mess' boring food tasted like a 5 star lunch.

It was almost 2 pm when we picked our cycles and left for coaching.

That was the first time ever in my life that I sat on the first bench with much enthusiasm.

Lekin bhaiya, wo kyu?

So the whole class, (even cute girls), could hear my 10th preparation journey when asked about it.

First class was mathematics. (*What a beautiful way to ruin a good mood*)

Sir came early and started scribbling on the board.

"WTF! Pagal ho gaya hai kya yeh?" my bench mate burst out. It was justified.

Come on, what kind of teacher doesn't ask about results on result day?

"Sir result! Sir result aaya hai aaj."

The whole class spat nothing but the word 'Result'.

And to our surprise, sir came up with the worst reply ever...

"Result? Tumhara koi test waghera hua tha kya coaching mein?"

"Yeh sahi mei pagla gaya hai," I agreed with my bench mate.

Our results had come and sir didn't even bother to care the least.

"Nahi sir, aaj 10th ka result aaya hai," someone shouted from behind with o hopes.

"Acha, sahi hai." said sir. *"Chalo khade ho jao jiske aaye hai 10 gpa/cpa jo bhi kehte ho tum log."*

A spark of electricity ran down my body...

Suddenly, I felt myself growing and growing, just like Hulk, my body with unparalleled energy rising from the chair.

It seemed the world was made only for me, to appreciate and adore my intelligence.

I felt like a **GOD**!

But reality slapped me hard when I looked behind, only to find the whole class standing.

"*Shabbash,*" sir finally spoke.

"*Poori class ne jhande gaad diye iss baar toh. Tumhare ghar waale bhi soch rahe honge ki IIT toh nikal hi jaaegi ab, haina? Chalo, take your seat everyone.*"

The look of disappointment on everyone's face spread faster than Covid.

"*Sir, aap khush nahi ho?*" asked a student, expecting a page-long appreciation for his results.

Sir paused, emotionless, and finally spoke, "*Dekho bacho, mei tumhe na toh chane ke jhaad par chadhana chahta hu aur na hi discourage karna chahta hu but reality yeh hai ki aapke 10th ke marks se 0.1% bhi yeh decide nahi hota ki aapka IIT/NEET me selection hoga ya nahi."*

Sir took a deep breath because he knew he'd hurt us.

"Yaha kota mei jab result aata hai na toh har dusre bache ke 10 CGPA hote hai, aur vo har bacha apne aap ko teacher se zyada samjhdaar sochne lagta hai.

Aur usi din se uss bache ki IIT/AIIMS mein jaane ke chances 0 ho jaate hai, 0."

What do you think happened after that?

Well bhaiya, I think sir ki bitching.

Correct.

"Sir apne aap ko bahut bada motivational speaker samjhte hai. Aaye bade Naala Sopara ke Sandeep Maheshwari," was one of the 1000 statements flying around the class.

"Sir ke khud ke ache number nahi aaye honge isliye humse jal rahe hai," was another.

Maths class got over and chemistry class began. And to give you some context, both maths and chemistry teachers were exact opposites of each other.

One was fire and the other, water.

As expected, the chemistry sir flaunted the brilliance of his students' minds and instantly became everyone's favourite.

"Yeh hota hai asli teacher...," said the class, while being on cloud 9.

"...jo bacho ki achievements par unhe aage ke liye motivate karta hai naa ki pichle waale sir ki tarah jo demotivate hi karta rehata hai har baat par."

But we were terribly wrong here...

11th June, 2017

"IIT jaana hai toh apne study room ki diwar formula sheets, bullet points, aur 'Target 99+ percentile and Double-Digit Advance rank' jaise statements se bhar do," said our coaching's HOD, coldly.

Our coaching had organised an orientation session (*saari fees toh yeh inhi faltu kaamo mai uda dete hai*) for us and our HOD was quite adamant in teaching the students about some **'Golden Points'.**

He believed a topper was just an average student who knew how to properly implement those 'Golden Points'.

"Jab bhi," said our HOD, *"jab bhi tumhara padhai ke alawa dusri faaltu cheezon mein mann lagne lage, toh inn golden points ko padhna. Tumhe pata chal jayega tum kaha kya galtiyan kar rahe ho."*

There are 2 types of students in this world:

Ones, who jot down everything their teachers say,

And the others who never.

What category do you think I fell into at that time?

Umm bhaiya, shayad 1st?

No, the second one. My ego was bigger than Ranbir Kapoor's dating list.

"Wohi ghisi piti psychological gyan aur motivational points likhva denge. Mai nahi likh raha," I said, ignoring every advice our HOD gave.

Kya aapko pata hai ek bache ki 11th barbaad hone ka sabse bada reason kya hota hai?

This overconfidence...

This might feel a bit off-topic but a human craves appreciation all the time.

You, me, your uncle, even your uncle's mausi ... everyone craves appreciation.

Remember how we made our chemistry teacher a hero after he appreciated our results?

If I do the same right now with you, the whole purpose of writing this book — which we'll eventually reveal — will fail.

I WILL FAIL!

So bhaiya, shouldn't we celebrate good results?

You should meri jaan, 100%, but...

But never ever cross **THE LINE** in overconfidence that I did ... and which still haunts me till this day.

'Self-confidence ek taraf and chane ke jhaad pe chadhna ek taraf!'

I scored well in the coaching's entrance test and my parents thought, *"Chalo ab toh IIT nikal hi jaayega."*

I topped in 10*th* and my parents thought, "*Chalo ab toh IIT nikal hi jaayega.*"

"Chalo ab toh IIT nikal hi jaayega," — ***"Chalo ab toh IIT nikal hi jaayega,"*** — ***"Chalo ab toh IIT nikal hi jaayega,"*** — ***"Chalo ab toh IIT nikal hi jaayega,"***

This is how you get **BARBAAD**. This is how I got **BARBAAD**.

And if at any point in life you feel that your:

- Parents don't get you

- Teachers don't get you

- Friends don't get you

And you find yourself going down the *barbaadi track...*

Then simply open this book and start reading each page thoroughly with patience and focus ... deeply understanding the gravity and meaning of every word.

So, are you ready to immerse yourself in the most amazing journey of your life – and begin its **UNBARBAADI**?

1
'$\{1^{st}, 2^{nd}, 3^{rd}, \ldots, 10^{th}\}$ v/s 11th'

"Bhai physics vale teacher ne half-yearly mei fail kar dia!" exclaimed my topper friend from my hometown over the phone ... who was crying with guilt, regret, and shame.

"Wtf !! Bhai tu toh topper tha 10th tak, tujhe kya ho gaya??" I replied in shock.

"Pata nahi bhai, 10th class tak sab badiya chal raha tha. 11th me toh duniya hi palat gayi hai. Ab toh na teacher bhao de rahi hai aur na hi Simran..."

It's very rare to find toppers sharing such traumatic experiences.

I mean, these things mostly happen with backbenchers, right?

Yes bhaiya, yeh topper kabse fail hone lag gaye? Aur agar inka yeh haal hai toh mera kya hoga?

I too passed my half yearly with margin marks. And not just me. This was the case with almost everyone in my class.

And even though we were studying just like we did in 10th, we still couldn't figure out what was wrong.

I'm not kidding.

Lemme tell you my daily routine I followed. Try finding any mistakes in it...

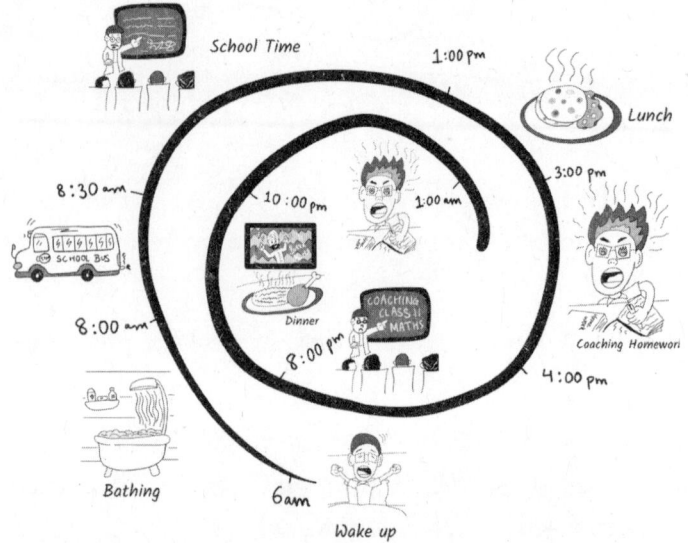

Found any? Nope, right?

This is how I studied… This is how you study… This is how most students study.

But that's not just it.

Another habit students carry from 10th to 11th (blindly) is – **'Copying homework and assignments from friends'.**

And it looks something like this:

There's a table. And it has 3 materials on it:

1. The Module to the right to read the questions

2. The Class Notes to the left for copying the methods teachers taught in class

3. The Homework Notebook in the centre for writing the answers

Now, this looks normal, right?

Yes bhaiya, sab kuch normal hi lag raha hai.

Well, here's a surprise for you...

If you continue following this same routine then you'll lack behind in your higher classes.

It's not your fault you follow this.

Now when our own Education System considers only those questions as **'IMPORTANT'** that repeatedly come in exams, then you don't have any choice but to copy and cram them up.

And even though *'rattafication'* and *'copying'* works just fine till 10th, their side effects start to appear later.

But bhaiya, padhai karne ka toh ek hi tareeka hota hai. Jaise 10th mein kiya waise 11th mein kyu nahi kar sakte?

The reason is...

10th has limited syllabus, unlike 11th.

Fewer concepts... Fewer topics... And fewer questions.

You can easily score good marks by just studying and revising the important stuff.

And as syllabus is less, this method does wonders. You do score good marks in your 10th.

But, but, but...

If, even by mistake, you follow this same study method in your 11th, then be ready to tell your story of *'Aise Hui Meri 11th Barbaad'* to your juniors.

Lekin bhaiya, wo kyu?

> *11th class ke pehle ek mahine me hi app itne sawal kar loge, jitne aapne 1st to 10th combined mein bhi nahi kiye honge.*

Even 'unlimited' doesn't justify the number of questions 11th throws at you.

As soon as you enter your 11th, you'll notice yourself transitioning from;

'Yeh 2 questions NCERT ke bahar se aaye the'

to

'Itne questions solve kar liye hai ki konsa question kaha se aaya kuch pata nahi'.

And you'll also see yourself outgrowing these habits:

- *'Nahi samajh aa raha toh koi baat nahi, ratt lunga aur same chaap aaunga exam mein'* - How many will you cram? 10?, 20?, 50?, 100? – That's what an average 11th grader solves in a day per subject.

- *'Exam se 1 hafta pehle bhi padhai shuru kar di toh bhi 95% phod denge'* - Hearing this, even your teachers will be left speechless.

All newcomers make a big mistake starting their 11th.

You will too...

They think 11th flows like a cool breeze, just like 10th, smooth and chilling ... with no clue of the tornadoes waiting for them on the other end.

And if you're reading this book, you fall under either one of these 2 categories:

1. You're mistake aware

2. You're not mistake aware

It doesn't matter what category you fall into.

What matters is whether you know how to use this problem to your advantage or not.

Ab bhaiya, sirf darate hi rahoge ya solution bhi bataoge?

Dara nahi raha meri jaan, aware kar raha hu... Despite having unlimited questions, 11th has 'limited' concepts.

And focusing and putting your energy into mastering those 'concepts' will help you score more, faster, and with less effort.

Bhaiya but ye 'concepts' kya hota hai ??

Let's discuss.

2

'Shah Rukh Khan: The Don / TCS Sir'

Using the routine I showed you in the previous chapter, I somehow managed to pass my half-yearly.

But still, it wasn't enough and didn't take me long to realise I was f****d.

I had 0 control over 2 things:

1. Class Notes: First 3 months of 11th witnessed me copying notes from my friend and the remaining 3 witnessed me saying:

- yaar yeh teacher ko koi train pakadni hai kya, itna tezz kyu bol raha hai?

- bhai mujhe samaj nahi aa raha notes banane pe dhyaan du ya simran pe?

- yeh sab faltu mehnat hai. Topper ke notes lunga aur full score karunga.

2. Revision: Revision and I shared the same relationship as Archana Puran Singh shared with The Kapil Sharma Show — *matlab shunya*. Effective revision without good class notes was not possible.

I was badly stuck in that situation. And it had its own consequences.

What do you think happened to me in my coaching?

Bhaiya, I think aapke coaching tests ke marks drop kar gaye honge ... yaa aapke backlog lag gaye honge. Right?

Right, but not 100%. There was something more to this.

Something that came as a nightmare and snatched away my whole confidence. So terrifying that it shattered me from within.

And it took me a lot of time and courage to get back up on my feet.

But bhaiya, what happened exactly?

I was demoted to the lowest batch of my coaching due to my constant poor performance in classes.

Straight away from A2 to C7. Shocking, right?

This literally broke me — threw me into the vicious cycle of DEPRESSION.

A 16 year old boy fighting this society's demons all by himself, all alone.

And I became bald.

Now, lower batches have 2 types of students:

1. Padhai jaisi moh maya se uth chuke hai.	1. Padhai toh jaan lagakar kar rahe hai lekin result nahi aa raha.
2. Dinbhar bas sutta, daaru, aur ladki baazi mein lage rehte hai.	2. Banda/Bandi ke naam pe 'B' tak nahi hota inki zindagi mein.
3. Baap ka paisa udaane mein koi bhi kasar nahi chodte.	3. Baap ka paisa inka bhi udd raha hai lekin books, crash courses, and health pe.
4. JEE/NEET toh door, inse boards bhi paas ho jaaye toh bahut badi baat hai.	4. Inhe bas ek chota sa hint ya roadmap chahiye aur yeh life ka har level cross kar lenge.

You, me, and most of us reading this book fall under the 2nd category who are ambitious but a little lost.

And as Don said, "*Agar kisi cheez ko dil se chaho ... toh puri kainaat usse tumse milane ki koshish mein lag jaati hai.*"

From '*reel to real*', this line became true when on a random Tuesday we were informed about the sudden change of our physical chemistry teacher and abse 'TCS Sir' would teach the subject.

The whole class was gossiping when a 5'6", semi-long haired, 24-year-old IITian wearing black blazer and dark blue Levi's jeans with white chunky sneakers entered the room and walked up directly to the blackboard.

'Chkk-chkkk' — the blackboard screeched as the IITian wrote 'THERMODYNAMICS' on it.

"Sab apni notebook ka kora page khol lo aur yeh heading daal do, aur haa, badi-badi heading daalna warna yeh chapter chamkega nahi." he said, studying the notes in his hands.

All excited, feeling his energy and imagining his lifestyle as an IITian, we started writing.

30 minutes later, our notebooks and the blackboard were filled with formulas, questions, theories, and God knows what.

The corners of my copy had tic-tac-toe games that screamed my bench-mate's inexpertise — *what a noob ;)*

We all were tired. Our hands were trembling with pain and our pens were soaked with sweat.

"Bas itne mai hi thak gaye kya? Abhi toh picture shuru hui hai meri jaan!" — sir said, realising he was a little too harsh on us.

"Chalo! Ab sab apni eyes close kar lo. Maine abhi tak jitna padhaya hai uska revision karvata hu."

We all closed our eyes and paid 100% attention to sir's words.

"Dekho sabse pehle hamne heading daali system, surroundings, and boundary — jisme humne padha ki system hota hai specific part of universe jiski hume study karni hoti hai; surroundings hota hai everything external to system and boundary hota hai something that separates system and surroundings. Next hamne padha First Law Of Thermodynamics jisme hamne formula padha $W = F.dx$ ...."

The class followed together and in just 5-7 minutes, we had collectively recalled the whole lecture — all thanks to his vibrant energy and dedication.

"Yeh toh kuch alag hi type feel hua bhaisahbbbbb, sab yaad ho gaya...

...vaah TCS vaah!!!", we all cheered collectively.

"Jo strategy mai ab tumhe btane jaa raha hu ussai tum JEE kya duniya ka koi bhi competitive exam aasani se phodd sakte ho," said sir.

"Dekho, ab ghar jaana aur ek baar notes mai karvaye hue sawal bina dekhe khud solve karne ki koshish karna aur saari theory ek baar yaad karke notes band karke soo jaana," he continued.

"Sir thodi saans toh le lo," a backbencher whispered.

Sir continued forward, *"Next din subah uthte hi ek rough page lena aur jaise abhi recall karna sikhaya waise recall karna aur saath mein page par likhte rehna. And boom, tumhari theory ab ekdum pakki ho gayi hai!"*

Bhaiya, kya yeh aapne try kiya, and if yes, then did it work?

Yes, I tried it and, to my surprise, it worked.

The next day, I remembered everything sir had taught and could solve most of my homework questions.

And you know what?

When I used this strategy to revise my notes, I realised I wasn't making good notes at all.

(good notes — notes that have every important word that comes out of your teacher's mouth even if it's a simplified version of a bookish definition).

But bhaiya, it's impossible to note everything and pay attention to the teacher at the same time. Multitasking is the root cause of lower marks, haina?

Haa meri jaan, sabar rakh. Bta raha hu. Lekin yeh technology India ke bahar nahi nikalni chahiye ;)

I too faced this problem. It's impossible to note everything and pay attention to the teacher at the same time.

But tumhare bhaiya ke paas tumhari har ek problem ka solution hai.

I owned a 1000 rupees ka button-wala phone.

And so every time I was in class ... I used to turn on the voice recorder ... record the whole lecture ... note down whatever I could without losing my focus and attention ... and complete the remaining notes by listening to the recording in my hostel room at 2x speed.

Lekin bhaiya, aisa kab tak karte rahenge? Yeh hamara saara time khaa lega. Phir hum DPPs and mock tests kab solve karenge?

Ok. I'll explain this with an example.

You don't see anything on day 1 of the gym. The body takes time to show results. And it happens only because of consistent efforts.

Just like that, you will find it difficult — nearly impossible — to make notes the way I suggested.

But after 1-1.5 months, you'll see a humongous increase in your concentration levels and note-taking abilities.

And then meri jaan, you can proudly ditch this method and start making notes while paying attention to your teacher at the same time.

But guess what, despite knowing and following this method, my 11th still got *Barbaad!*

Wo kaise bhaiya?

Let's discuss the 'how' behind this in detail in the next chapter...

3
'Raksha Bandhan'

Life never fails to bless you with little sparks.

Sparks of intense motivation that force you to change your life overnight.

'Aaj puri raat padhunga aur saara syllabus cover karunga.'

'Subah 4 baje ka alarm set karunga aur 12 ghante padhunga.'

'Pura din phone off rakhunga aur social media detox karunga.'

You might have felt these sparks at least once in your life — and you're feeling one right now – to complete this book and use it to leave 99% of your competition behind.

I too felt one in 11th...

And that feeling was strong.

And what followed was a series of events and results that I still feel proud of till this very day.

I had just learnt TCS sir's revision method when, in a day, my whole hostel got empty.

It was Raksha Bandhan and coaching was off for 3 days.

Students had already booked their tickets to home.

But I didn't.

And a crazy idea flashed in my mind...

I dialled my phone and said, *"Mummy, mai ghar wapis nahi aa raha. Hostel rehke 3 din sirf revise karunga aur agle test mai ache marks laaunga."*

And *phir kya*, 2 *gaali khayi* and the very next second I was staring at 4 thick books lying on my study table.

Hey, did I tell you about Krish? No, not the one with the ugliest mask ever.

Krish was my good friend; ICSE 10th topper and a straight 'A' student.

My conversation with mummy over-fuelled him with motivation.

And guess what? Even he denied to go back home!

At least I had some company now.

The next 3 days felt so powerful. I promise, I could've easily beaten Thanos alone.

-Anti-Kumbhkaran Sleeping:

2 hours of sleep. 4 hours of non-stop studying. Then repeat.

We both helped each other kyunki hitting the snooze button felt tempting. And so when he was sleeping, I was studying and vice-versa.

-The Zandu Balm:

At times, sleep kicked in so hard we often lost control of it. So, Krish and I began applying balm on our foreheads and tied them up with *rumaals*.

This helped with 2 things — decreased yawns and increased concentration.

- The Berozgaar Diet:

We stopped eating roti aur chawal and survived only on Coffee and Parle-Gs. Our idea was to eliminate everything that deprived our body of its precious energy.

Papa kaha karte the ki – *"jitna heavy khaoge, shareer ko utni hi energy usai digest karne mein deni hogi, toh jab tumhari energy vaha par lagegi toh neend zaroor aaegi."*

-Decorated Hostel Walls ... But With A Twist:

While other hostel rooms had walls filled with posters of you know what — *(aaj blue hai paani paani paani paani paani paani, aur din bhi ... umm, let's not go there)* — our walls only had formulas and equations, so we never had an excuse for not revising.

-Quality Poop-Time:

Our toilets saw more of our notes and less of our bums in those 3 days.

Maa kasam, we had become so involved and dedicated that even if we dreamt...

...(while sleeping only for 2 hours, which was a miracle), our dreams only had us running before 'X's***************and not 'EX's.

Even my mom told me she had once called in the morning and the convo began with, *"Hello Shobhit, uthjaa nashta miss mat karna aaj bhi,"*...

...and I had replied, *"Haa iss sawal ke shuru mein hi agar 'x' ki value put kar doge toh complicated ho jaayega isiliye end mein hi put karna."*

We had soaked in and digested every word from our class notes and scribbled 1 entire notebook by solving DPPs and homework problems, HC Verma, and a ton of PYQs — in just 3 freaking days!

We had a test just after this Raksha Bandhan Break.

And we slept for just 90 mins before test day ... to go through each and every formula, twice.

Later in the afternoon of the test day, I was in my room calculating marks from the answer key.

And 115 marks later I ran to Krish's room.

"Kya bhai 360 mein se 360 phod diye kya?" asked Krish, amazed by my electrifying energy.

"Arey nahi 115 ban rahe hai," I replied, with a tear or two in my eyes while hugging him.

If it weren't for him I couldn't have pulled off this much hard work.

"Farak nahi padhta aapke marks kitne aa rahe hai. Farak isse padhta hai ki kya tumne apna 100% diya ya nahi," we both shouted, remembering the invaluable advice our teachers gave.

I was satisfied...

Not because I had scored 115 but because in the past 3 days I had given my best ... my fullest ... my. 100%. 110% in fact.

Now, that tiny little spark had turned into a well-lit fire and the passion to work hard was at its peak.

Every student in the radius of 1 km now knew of a *'taklu'* from room 108 who was studying like a maniac.

I used to keep my door open so if somehow I slept, someone walking through the corridor would spot me and wake me up.

Khaana, nahana, hagna, dosto ke room par jaana, movies dekhna, games khelna, aur even ghar pe call karna ... all felt like big time wasters.

That was the level of *pagalpanti* I had achieved.

But bhaiya, yeh sab healthy nahi hota, right?

Not fully aware about the physical part but mentally, this shit is not at all healthy.

I'll tell you why...

You know, when you work hard, you put yourself at the pinnacle and the rest of the world seems naive.

Your thoughts and opinions feel superior and you fail to acknowledge a simple thing — you fail to take in suggestions and feedbacks.

This was exactly the case with me. I failed to acknowledge feedback as I committed mistakes in my journey.

One day, I was having lunch with Shailendra — he was the replica of Siddharth Malhotra from Student of the Year.

The perfect all-rounder type who managed to study, play, gossip, and have fun, all in just 24 hours, and who was among my first friends in Kota.

He was enjoying Nora Fatehi's performance while I was awfully trying to finish my food asap (as mentioned earlier, eating food was a waste of time).

"*Shobhit bhai dekh bura mat maanio,*" said Shailendra, in an extremely slow and concerned voice, "*acha dost hai tu isiliye bol raha hu — aise gadho ki tarah padhne se kuch nahi hoga.*"

I was confused...

Was he calling me a *gadha* because of my *taklu* head or was he serious?

"*Jab tak tu smart work nahi karega...*" continued Shailendra, "*...tab tak kuch bhi fayda nahi hoga.*

Aise bas 'naam ke liye' hw complete karna, modules aur dpp solve karna, revision karna, inn sab se kuch nahi hone wala," he completed, lifted his plate, and left.

"*Arey, but yeh toh batate ja ki smart work hota kya hai? Faaltu ka lecture suna ke chala gaya,*" I exhaled, sounding like a typical UP guy with paan stuffed in his mouth.

I reflected over Shailendra's words for 20 seconds straight until I couldn't.

"*Theek hai nahi pata mujhe smart work toh mai gadho ki tarah hard work karta rahunga.*" I sighed, bitterly.

"*Padhai hi kar raha hu unlike others jo bass time waste kar rahe hai. Yeh intentionally bolke gaya mujhe. Isko bass apna competition kam karna hai.*"

I left the mess, returned to my room, and continued my studies.

November 17...

11th had nearly come to an end. And for the diwali party my 3 Gujarati friends had invited me to their hostel.

One was in the top batch of our coaching and is in IIT Kharagpur right now.

The second one was in the second top batch and is in PDPU right now.

The third one is busy with his own passion projects nowadays.

I was truly upset with my previous hostel vibes. And as expected, I felt a wave of optimism as soon as I stepped in theirs.

Immediately, after gossiping with my topper friend, I noticed some differences:

- Jaha mai 100 books padhta tha, yeh insaan sirf coaching modules ki puja karta tha.

- Jaha mai sirf 4 ghante sota tha, yeh aaram se 7-8 ghante ki neend leta tha.

- Jaha maine khaana khaane tak ko time waste declare kar diya tha, yeh insaan 1-2 ghante badminton bhi khelta tha.

- Aur surprisingly, iski girlfriend bhi thi. Aur yeh roz nahata bhi tha, damnnn!

And despite doing all that, he was still in our coaching's top batch!

That means, something was off that kept me from achieving extraordinary results.

Papa kaha karte the, *"Kuch baatein instantly samaj nahi aati, dheere dheere uska matlab samajh aata hai."*

Shailendra's words hit me ... and they hit me hard.

Yes I was doing hw... I was solving modules and DPPs... I was constantly revising notes...

But for the mere sake of it.

Every goddamn thing I was doing, all of a sudden, felt like a plain formality.

- Giving priority to revision of notes ONLY and not focusing on the other important tasks — hw, mock tests, and whatnot.

- And even if I touched hw problems, I would only solve the ones that felt easier, circling the others. (*Aur Vo gole aaj bhi gole hi hai*).

Also, I would rarely ask doubts and would ignore if someone else asked the same.

- Plus, I saw students solving thick refresher books wildly. And that made me buy a few. But I never actually solved even one completely.

Remember I told you how a person is always hungry for appreciation.

"Arey kitna padhega? Padh padh ke pagal ho jaayega kya?" were comments from almost everyone who saw me studying.

And that made me feel really good.

It had become some kind of a 'show off' for me — showing people I study a lot ... solving a shit ton of books ... always saying no to fun.

And that cost me my effectiveness.

Hopping from one book to another had become my new habit.

I solved questions of only those topics I was strong at and never paid attention to clearing up my doubts.

If you're able to solve questions, it means you have a strong foot in that particular topic.

And if you're not, it means, there's still plentiful studying left to do.

My problem was I never touched questions from topics I was weak at.

And so I never focused on my weaknesses and lingered on with questions from only stronger topics.

And thanks to my arrogance, I never saw this as a problem and kept on working hard like a GADHA.

Hamesha yaad rakhna: Half knowledge is devastating.

Toh bhaiya, aapne kiya kya?

Kya karta? Boriya bistar uthaya aur inke hostel mein shift ho gaya!

Cherry on the cake — My hostel room was in front of this topper friend's room.

And then began my journey of: ***'11ᵗʰ Barbaad se 12ᵗʰ Aabaad'.***

But bhaiya, aapke iss topper friend ka naam toh bta do...

4

'Zeel Patel'

And then I opened his notebook and module ... *aur meri aankhe fati ki fati reh gayi.*

Lekin bhaiya, aisa kya tha usme?

Khichdi!!! Aur vo bhi desi ghee mein doobi hui!!

Matlab bhaiya? Samajh nahi aaya?

Every question in his module had a page number written on it.

"Har question pe jo page number hai, wo notebook ke uss page ko point karta hai jispai maine usai attempt kiya hai," said Zeel, figuring out the confused look on my face.

"Agar sawal complete ho gaya," Zeel continued, *"toh usai tick kar deta hu warna gola lagakar 1-2 ghante baad firse try karta hu. Tab bhi nahi hua toh class mein doubt puch leta hu."*

But bhaiya, page number ke peeche ka logic kya hai?

It had 2 crucial benefits, (applies to your preparation as well), according to Zeel:-

1. During revision, it became easier for him to find solutions to the questions he couldn't solve.

Lekin bhaiya, solution toh Google pe bhi mil jayega. Toh itna sab kyu?

True, you can find everything on Google. Plus, there's ChatGPT now too.

But there are 2 issues:

- There's no guarantee the method you'll find on the internet and the method your teacher suggests are same. This causes confusion. And confusion leads to drop in your interest and exam scores.

- Also, you never realise how looking for answers turns into an hour long scrolling session. This is disastrous. Distractions for a serious student like you are disastrous.

2. The second benefit? Ease of asking doubts. He could tell his teacher exactly where he was stuck — by referring to the page number — and then reattempt it afterwards.

Zeel was incredibly dedicated as a 16-year-old student. His target was to get his doubts resolved within 12 hours.

And if by any reason, he couldn't clear them in class, you would find him flying around in the hostel, even at night, until he could turn all his 'golas' into tick marks.

Such little insignificant things create the biggest differences. They transform you from an average student into a topper.

Lemme tell you an interesting story:

Once upon a time, there was a village that experienced severe water shortage.

So, the Panchayat came up with a solution — to dig a well.

But no one knew where to start and where they would find enough water to quench villagers' needs.

Someone advised to start near a peepal ka ped and after 2 days of digging a 15 feet deep well, they found nothing.

Then someone advised to dig near the highway; still no luck. And then near the panchayat office; again nothing.

"*Alag alag jagah 15-15 feet ke gaddhe khodne se badhiya ek hi jagah 50 feet khod doge to paani mil jaayega,*" said an elderly after pitying over the villagers' bad luck.

And so following his words, everyone went on digging a deeper well, only to shed happy tears at 4 days of hard work and 45 feet deep well that, in no time, got filled with water.

Yes bhaiya, I'm getting what you mean.

Alright, tell me what is it then?

So bhaiya, what you're saying is:

'Aap 100-200 books ek shath solve kar rahe the lekin effectively nahi. Koi bhi book jab aap solve karne baithte the, toh sirf easy questions karte the aur baaki ko gola maar dete the.

Aap bass show off karne ke liye books pe books solve karte the and kisi aur ke pass agar koi new book dikhe toh usko bhi khareed lete the.

Iski jagah agar aapne 1 book par hi ache se focus kiya hota toh shayad aap aaj IIT mein hote.'

Waah, ek dum right.

Chalo, at least iss book se tumhe cheezon mein clarity toh aa rahi hai.

Ok, moving forward...

I remember having confidence (during my JEE) in only those chapters whose modules I had 100% completed.

And when questions from other chapters were thrown at me, I would literally piss my pants in fear and disgust of not being able to solve them.

But bhaiya, kya aapko nahi lagta...

- 2-3 times notes revise karna

- saara hw complete karna

- doubts ko reattempt karna

- regularly DPPs karna

...yeh sab ½ din mein karna impossible hai?

It's difficult, but not impossible.

Remember: Like a masterpiece, great things take time to come to life.

At first, the canvas seems cluttered with unfinished strokes, but as time passes, each detail falls into place, creating a breathtaking work of art.

And just like that, with patience and persistence, even the most challenging tasks become effortless, and success comes easy.

But still, you will fail if you...

Arey bhaiya, aisa toh mat bolo.

...if you don't do this **CONSISTENTLY!**

"Consistency is harder when no one is clapping for you"
~ Luis Garcia.

Tension, stress, backlogs, less scores, peer pressure, parental pressure, depression, movies, parties, sacrificing mobile — it takes a lot of courage to see results when you have problems flying all over your head.

As I always say:

[Gym jaane se instantly six packs nahi dikhte, pehle din ka dard alag.

Similarly, inn sab study techniques se instant results nahi dikhte, but if done consistently, toh ek dum se marks ki baarish hone lagti hai.]

Lekin bhaiya, agar itna sab karne ke baad bhi results na dikhe toh?

Toh phir tumhare room ki koi toh window khuli reh gayi hogi.

Iska matlab, Shobhit bhaiya?

Aao batata hu...

5
'Khuli Window'

I have a simple question for you.

Let's say you buy a brand new AC... And after turning it on, it fails to cool the room.

What do you check first?

Bhaiya, ki AC kharab toh nahi hai?

Close, try again.

Umm, nahi pata bhaiya.

Arey, ki koi khidki ya gate khula toh nhi reh gaya...

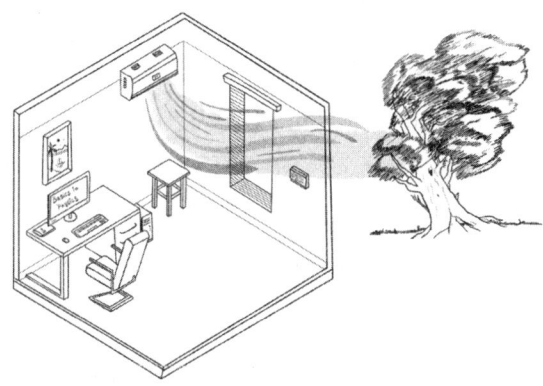

Likewise, if you don't see any results even after consistently following all your study techniques advised by your teachers and parents, (and even me)...

Then there might be some distractions pulling you back.

Same was the case with me.

One single addiction cost me thousands of rupees and my entire mental health.

I spent my complete 11th with a *'button waala phone'*.

And mid-way my 12th, JIO phone was released — it had internet, whatsapp, youtube, and literally everything a student would need to successfully waste their whole day.

Living without a smartphone (for 1.5 years) was like having a long distance relationship.

And so I became desperate ... desperate to have a smartphone just like my other friends.

Then what, I buttered my papa into believing that this phone would be an investment and we could video call over it.

And so just you know;

Jab bhooke sher ko ek sath bahut saara khana mil jaata hai toh woh hakka-bakka reh jaata hai.

Similarly, I got so addicted to that phone ki I would literally lie to my parents to get more data just to binge watch shows and movies all day long.

The situation became so worse that for every movie/show I watched, 1 backlog got added up to an already existing huge pile.

Alongside that, I stopped doing my hw and avoided the teacher's attention in class by keeping my head down.

But somehow, TCS sir noticed me and gave me a tight scolding — in front of everybody.

That day I realised my non-seriousness and regretted every bit of decision I took for 1 whole month.

And what happened next was something nobody I know of ever did in their life.

I returned to my hostel, and with burning rage and humiliation, crushed my phone under the legs of a steel chair.

Now don't get me wrong here. Nor think of me as a stupid psycho.

I'm not advising you to break your phones.

What I mean is if you get stuck in this vicious cycle today, you'd be crushed by your competition tomorrow.

Yes bhaiya, I feel mujh mein kaafi potential hai lekin mai usko effectively utilise nahi kar paa raha hu – just because of all these bloody distractions.

Correct.

So, without wasting a single second, let's list down all your major distractions…

...that act as hurdles in your path to achieving a seat in your dream college, and ultimately, making your parents proud!

- Toxic Relationships
- Porn Addiction
- Smoking Addiction
- Social Media Addiction
- Everything Gadget Addiction

All these distractions act as a source of leakage ... or shall we call it a 'Khuli Window' in your academic journey.

In the beginning, they weigh nothing.

But as time passes, their weight and pressure on your shoulders start to leave a heavy tax in your life, sucking in your energy and killing you off your motivation to study.

Bhaiya, aapne yeh to bta diya ki hamari life mein kya-kya distractions hai aur aayegi. Toh ab yeh bhi bata do ki unko tackle kaise karna hai.

The best way to not let these distractions stop you from claiming what is yours is your **MINDSET.**

Have a clear mindset of putting your exam prep as your absolute priority.

Rest all comes after that...

"*Yeh 2 saal aap tapasya pe aaye ho,*" our Kota teachers used to say.

"*Jaise rishi muni ki tapasya bhang karne ke liye rakshas kabhi tez barish karva dete the toh kabhi tez hawa chalwa dete the, opposite gender bhej dete the, iske bawajood, jo rishi muni inn sab distarctions se ladd kar, bina beheke, apni tapasya jaari rakhte the, wo hamesha safal hote the.*"

Same is the case for all students ... and same is the case for you.

In your path to achieving your goals, you'll be painfully greeted with a ton of irritating thorns (called distractions).

And your ability to face them without getting affected will determine your 'SAFALTA'.

I used to frequently get attracted to girls in Kota.

That's why I went bald — to remind myself that I looked insanely unattractive not only to date a girl but even to talk to one.

But bhaiya, yeh toh pagalpan hai.

Right, and this level of pagalpan is compulsory when you have big goals.

Every distraction will seem small or even fade away when you become pagal for that 1 thing that keeps you awake at nights ... all 365 days!

"Smartphone aapke selection ke chances 95% se kam kar deta hai," I stated while addressing students in a seminar at Kota.

"Throw it and button-wala phone mangwa lo."

And then the silent hall broke out into chaos and debates like a fish market. The children kept pointing towards a smartphone's importance.

They came up with some 'Bahane' as to why a smartphone is a necessity in their prep.

And I gave on-spot solutions to help with their confusions.

"Bhaiya coaching material and DPPs telegram pe aati hai toh bina phone ke access kaise karenge?"

My Answer:

1. For Hostelers- Strike out a deal with your hostel mates.

At least one will have a smartphone. Give them patties and coke in return for his phone (only Sundays).

And then, you can take printouts of your coaching material and DPPs.

Plus, spending money on patties, coke, and print-outs will not hurt as much as spending lacs on coaching institutes with no satisfactory results.

2. For Non-Hostelers- Get your parents/guardians' numbers added in your coaching group. That will do just fine...

"Bhaiya agar koi concept class mein samaj nahi aaye toh video lecture kaise dekhenge?"

My Answer: Smartphones in India came in the early 2000s. Students still cleared IIT/AIIMS/UPSC before.

If they can do it, you can too.

Lemme ask you a basic question – Why do you pay so much fees in your coaching?

To complete the syllabus?

Nope. Even YouTube helps you do that — for free.

You don't pay the fees for syllabus completion but for one-to-one guidance. To clear your doubts on the spot.

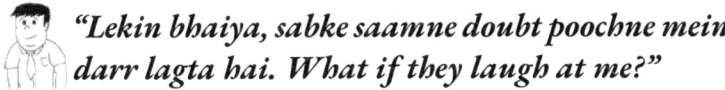
"Lekin bhaiya, sabke saamne doubt poochne mein darr lagta hai. What if they laugh at me?"

My Answer: Every student in your class is sailing in the same boat.

They are still preparing. Nobody has cracked anything yet.

"Doubt poochne se bacho ki duaeen milti hai," my teachers used to say.

"Tum jab ek doubt poochte ho toh uss samay 40-50 bacche aur hote hai jinka same doubt hota hai lekin poochne se darrte hai.

Toh agar tumne pooch liya toh duaeen hi milengi aur kya"

"Bhaiya meri classes toh online hoti hai. Bina smartphone ke it's not possible."

My Answer: You can use your parents/guardians' phone for that. No big deal.

This *Vaad-Vivaad* continued for 45 minutes and at least you know who lost the debate.

The Smartphone.

Long story short — If you keep your hand on your heart and ask yourself whether you seriously need a smartphone in your school life or not, the answer will always be 'NO' — **You don't need a phone.**

Lemme share one more real life incident.

We had an Assam state topper in our hostel.

- Highly talented

- Hardworking

- And a smart guy

It took him only 2 months to complete the entire 11th.

Crazy right?

We would start a chapter and he'd be done with its revision for the 4th time.

He was in the top-most batch of our coaching.

When 10th results came out and he was declared the state topper, his society head gifted him a laptop and a smartphone...

And from that day, his academics took an aggressive downfall.

He got so addicted to them that it led to his demotion from top to the lowest batch — that too, within a month.

He became a hunchback and even started bunking his classes.

And to make matters even worse ... he passed his 12th with just margin marks.

'Prevention is better than cure'. Everyone knows that and so do you.

Don't give yourself any chance to get distracted. Make friends... Have fun... And enjoy this beautiful phase.

Meet new people and talk to them. You'll miss these 2 years of slavery once you get into college.

"Dost ache toh bnao hi par jiske dost ho uske ache dost bano bhi," said Anubhav Singh Bassi, in one of his TEDx.

Because of the generational gap, your parents sometimes fail to understand you. *Isiliye aise samay par dost hi ek dusre ke sabse jyada kaam aate hai.*

But bhaiya, mai toh already addicted hu. Ab kya karu?

If you think you are addicted, clap for yourself first.

At least you understand your shortcomings and are ready to transform them.

But to actually help you out, here're some methods (that work):

1. Bhaad mein jaaye phone: Dedicate specific hours of your day for using the phone. And during other hours, live like a caveman.

Remember it shouldn't be the first thing you look at after waking up. This shoots up your dopamine levels and you find other, already boring tasks such as studying, more boring.

2. Mujhe disturb mat karo: Turn off all notifications for apps that distract you while studying. Social Media, games, news, etc.

These apps should not be allowed to hijack your focus and energy and steal your precious preparation time.

3. Masti karo, chill karo: Find activities you enjoy doing. Exercise, read, or talk, for a break from books. This will always make you feel better than a smartphone.

Important: Replacing old habits takes time and effort. Do you have the patience required?

6
'Ghar ki Murgi'

"Haa yaar, meri papa se baatcheet band hai aaj kal," my crush from Delhi said, casually.

It had been a while since I last spoke with her after arriving in Kota.

I rolled my eyes in disbelief. *"Wtf, aisa bhi hota hai kya?"*

Who does their father like that?

"Haa yaar vo papa ne meri ek dost ke insta ke through meri cafe ki stories dekh li."

"He saw I bunked coaching," she said, inflating a bubble out of her chewing gum.

"But yaar Shobhit tu hi bata, kya 24 ghante gadho ki tarah padhte rahe aur bilkul bhi masti na kare?

"Calm down. He's just concerned for you. Nothing else," I assured, trying to bring her temper down.

"Aisa kuch nahi hai. Arey hame bhi apni life dhang se jeene ka haq hai ya nahi?" she yelled, in pure frustration.

"Maine toh papa se bol diya hai — aapke help ki koi jarurat nahi, mai khud sambhal lungi,"

I was upset to hear that. This (in my friend circle) was new.

Cuz you learn the importance of your parents the moment you start living away from them.

"Mummy inn hostel waalo ne baalti bhi local di hai. Ab tum hi batao jab roz paani ka flow hota hai, phir bhi gandi kaise ho jaati hai?" I asked mumma over call after noticing some dirt built-up on the inside of my water bucket for the 5th consecutive day.

"Nahi beta, baalti ko bhi regularly saaf karna padhta hai," my mom replied, in the sweetest tone ever.

"Heinnnnnn?" I shouted, in total amazement. *"Par ghar pe toh humne kabhi saaf nahi ki!"*

"Kar deti thi beta main, bas tumhe kabhi pata nahi chalta tha."

Papa used to give me money for my expenses in Kota…

And during those days, spending even 10 rupees felt like *'bahut zayda kharche'*.

Because when you're with your parents, money flows like a river — *bill toh papa hi pay karte hai isiliye.*

But the biggest crime we commit is taking them for granted … or *'Ghar ki Murgi - Daal Barabar'.*

And side by side, we think of them as our biggest enemies. We feel they never let us live life on our own terms.

Take 2 sec out and think this through: Maybe all that your parents want for you is exactly the same as what you want for yourself.

Do you want to be successful?

And do your parents want you to be successful?

If the answer to both the questions is yes then why do you think of them as your enemies?

Our parents have the biggest goldmine — a wealth of **EXPERIENCE.**

They can spot the difference between genuine friends and selfish snakes just by looking at their faces.

Whenever I have a meeting, I bring my father along.

Maybe he doesn't understand Insta, Youtube, or Social media much.

Maybe he doesn't even understand anything in the whole meeting.

But he has always given me valuable advice on whether to have long-term collaborations with those I meet or not.

Here's a priceless learning that will not only help you in your student life but also in future too.

My 11th here in Kota started with papa doing surprise visits to check whether I was studying or just time-passing.

And always, either I was found studying or sleeping.

So, this created a sense of trust among my parents that I was sincere and was putting in continuous daily efforts.

They never scolded me for less marks cuz they knew I wasn't tricking them.

Your parents expect only 1 thing from you — that you study well — and that is *toh* bare minimum, right?

That you become stable in life so you never feel terrified whenever life throws lemons at you.

Once you build that trust, you can literally ask for anything.

I did the same and my parents supported my decision of following my passion and skipping college placements.

Alright. Imagine you're playing gully cricket and a new player enters. How do you judge him? How do you form opinions about him?

By looking at his previous performances.

Right?

Similarly, you'll be judged on your past performances in life ... 10th, 12th, college, placements, and almost everything in between.

The trust you build TODAY as a student will help you put your personal interests and passion on your parents' table TOMORROW ... without any arguments.

Going to some cafe in the name of tuition will not only upset them, but will also cost you their faith.

"*Beta serious ho jao.*" I know you're tired of hearing these words.

But once your parents gain trust, they'll never nod their heads in disgust around you ... **NEVER!**

And I'm a living proof for this statement. My parents said yes to every career diversion I made — simply because they trust me.

Or you can say, I built that trust.

But bhaiya, parents ka chalta hai lekin what about relatives?

Woh toh hamesha taane hi dete rehte hai. Unko yeh passion-vaishan kuch samaj nahi aata.

Unka kya kare?

Chalo aao, batata hu...

7

'Bahar Ke Dogale'

Do you remember this program: ***'Saas Bhi Kabhi Bahu Thi'***?

I still have faint memories of me and my family leaving all work and tasks and sitting together at 9pm dot just to disappear into the beauty of this show.

But why was it so popular?

It's because they knew what viewers wanted to watch.

They created a show almost every Indian household could relate to.

"Iski saas bilkul meri saas ki tarah hai. Daayan kahi ki," an Indian bahu lashes out every time she sees *Kalesh* unfold in that program.

My papa used to repeat the same sentences over and over every time any relative asked him about my academic status.

Relative: *"Bhaisahab, Shobhit kya kar raha hai aaj kal?"*

Papa: *"Areey bhaisahab, kya batau, yeh ladka toh haath se nikal gaya.*

Maine to IIIT mein padhne bheja tha, pata nahi kya video vagarah banane lag gaya.

Meri to sunta bhi nahi hai ab, isliye maine bol diya ki joh karna hai kar apni life hi barbaad karega."

But why bhaiya, aap toh YouTube par itna acha kar rahe ho, fir bhi aapke papa aap se khush nahi hai?

Bahut khush hai! Infact ye book likhne ka idea bhi unhi ka tha.

Bade log ek baat kehte hai na — 'nazar lag jaaegi' — vaise toh I don't believe in superstitions but the logic behind this is true.

Lemme explain!

"Aur beta, padhai kaisi chal rahi hai?" — sounds familiar?

Whenever any of your relatives ask you this question and you reply with *'Achi chal rahi hai'*...

...do you really think they feel happy within?

Aji Ghanta.

They'll only be happy when you have fights in your home similar to *'Saas Bahu Aur Saazish's'*, and even financial struggles.

They'll enjoy eating your sweets when you share your successes with them — securing top ranks, cracking exams, buying cars and houses — *but andar hi andar woh jalenge.*

So, if they never actually vouch for your growth and betterment, why bother telling them anything?

Because no matter what you achieve, they'll still be jealous of your life's upward trajectory.

You know what?

Relatives, school friends, and even my crush didn't know I was going to Kota for my jee prep.

"Naani gaav mein akeli rehti hai, toh unke paas rehne ke liye school change kiya," used to be my go-to excuse to anyone questioning my transfer decision.

And do you know this is also one of top reasons for frequent suicide cases in Kota.

Relative's continuous *'Bass, nikal gayi hawa?'*, *'Hame toh pata tha ki nahi ho paayega isse'*, has tortured countless innocent souls who, though late in life, but at least realised IIT/NEET was not for them.

And these mean taunts bring nothing but a drop in self-confidence and a lack of motivation to hustle even harder.

Plus they feel they've failed their parents — shattered their dreams of seeing their child in news interviews — all this at such a young age.

But lemme assure you, everyone except your parents are **DOGALE**.

It won't take these dogale people much time transitioning from *'Maine bola hi tha isse kuch nahi ho paaega'* to *'Maine toh bola hi tha yeh kuch bada zaroor karega'*.

Chapters Over — Hall Started

I used to live in a joint family during my childhood.

Everyone in my family had separate rooms...

Tauji-Taiji had one room, Chachu-Chachi had one, and another one for my parents.

Toh bhaiya, aap kaha sote the?

All the remaining kids with my younger unmarried Chachu used to sleep in the HALL (basically the drawing room of our house, which was too big to be called a room, so we named it 'hall').

Btw, have you guys ever made *'Joote ke dabbe se ghar'* in your childhood days?

I was a big DIY fan.

One day, my *chachu* gifted me a pair of sneakers ... but more than that, I was excited for the cardboard box of those shoes.

I immediately rushed to my room and started making a house using it.

And for denoting members in each room, I used old pens.

I picked 2 pens and put them in one room saying, *"Yeh tauji-taiji ka room,"*...

Then took another 2 pens and put them in the second room saying, *"Yeh bade chachu-chachi ka room,"*...

And when all the rooms got full, I took the remaining pens and put them all in the drawing room, saying, *"Aur baaki sab gaye hall mein."*

The point is, all the remaining people would fit inside the hall of our home.

Similarly, I've named this chapter 'Hall' which contains all the remaining yet highly important topics/problems that we left in the previous chapters.

Just navigate to the hall that has your particular problem, and you will, without any difficulty, find the right solution for it.

Hall - A: 'Tests'

This is the only million-dollar advice I got from my teachers in Kota:

Never revise for your tests...

Till 10th, we're told to revise one night prior to every test (*chahe class test ho ya final exams*).

But they never teach us when and how to revise in higher classes.

My first coaching test in class 11th had 10 chapters in syllabus.

And so I revised them all.

Next test had 16 chapters.

And so I revised them all.

Next had 22...

And then 25...

And then 30...

Revising 30 chapters one night before the test is not at all possible!

And even if somehow you manage to pull it off, you'll either remember in bits and pieces or get a headache writing the test.

This taught me a valuable lesson — Do not revise before your exams (unless they're finals).

I had become way too casual during my test preparation.

Tests se 2 ghante pehle pata chalta tha ki aaj test hai !!

Give your regular tests as surprise tests just to see whether you're able to retain concepts or not.

The second blunder I made was post test analysis.

I never analysed my...

- silly mistakes,
- strategies of attempting questions,
- how I chose what questions to leave,
- and what sections to solve first,

...for my first half of 11th.

Cause till my 10th, I was a 90+ scorer. So there wasn't much to analyse.

But as soon as you enter 11th ... the scenario changes completely.

Higher classes involve:
- different attempting strategies
- different leaving strategies
- different solving strategies

Everything is different from 11th onwards...

Q1. *To bhaiya fir tests ki analysis karne ka best tarika kya hai?*

Sol. See, for every 100 students who give tests, only 2-3 perform post test analysis. And these are the same students you see on institute posters doing a '✌' after their results.

Lekin bhaiya, test dena ke baad dimaag kharab ho jaata hai...

Thakaan alag hoti hai... Bilkul acha nahi lagta analysis karna!

There's a very beautiful quote that says:

"Nahi acchi lagne vaali cheezo ko karne se hi acchi lagne vaali cheeze milegi."

So this is how you make sure you are on one of those posters too.

Take a diary and make a flowchart.

Start by writing 'Test Analysis' on top.

Now you'll have two categories:

The ones that gave you a '+4' and the ones that gave you a '-1.'

For all the questions that gave you a '+4', it simply means your understanding of that particular topic is top-notch.

So, no need to analyse this section.

The '-1' category is where scope of improvement lies.

Alright. On it then...

Under the '-1' category, do this... 2 arrows from each side mentioning 'Attempted But Incorrect' on one and 'Not Attempted' on another.

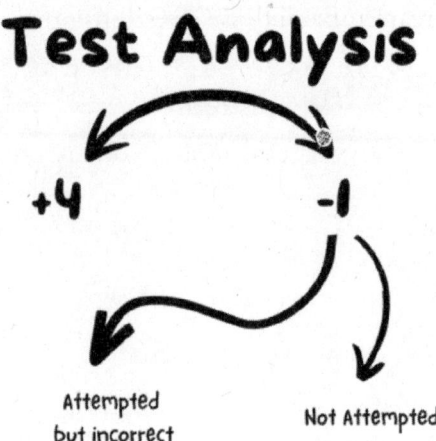

Now, under the **'Attempted'** category, write all the reasons for the questions you solved incorrectly.

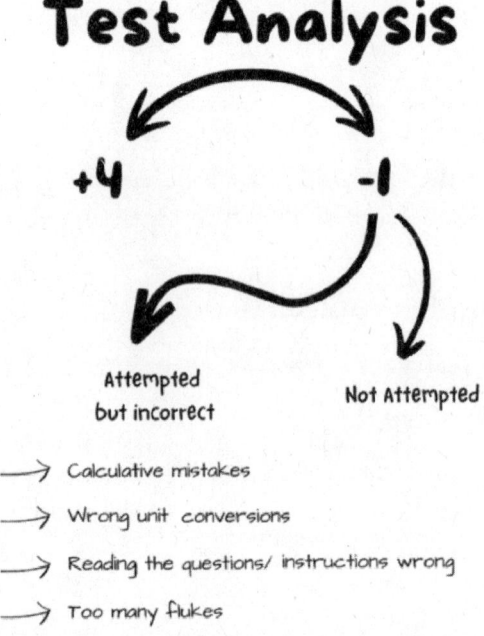

Now, reattempt all those questions once again......

yes, once again.

But Bhaiya, ussei kya hoga?

2 things will happen now:

- either you'll solve them correctly

- or you'll not and get stuck again

If it's the first case then congrats, you just levelled up.

If not then here's what you need to do...

Go back to the topic and revise it once. Then attempt the question again. If you solve it then congrats, and if not then repeat the process until you get them all right.

Coming back to the 2nd category — the **'Not Attempted'** one.

This category is much more important. The top rankers are generally the ones who tackle and correctly solve the questions from this particular category.

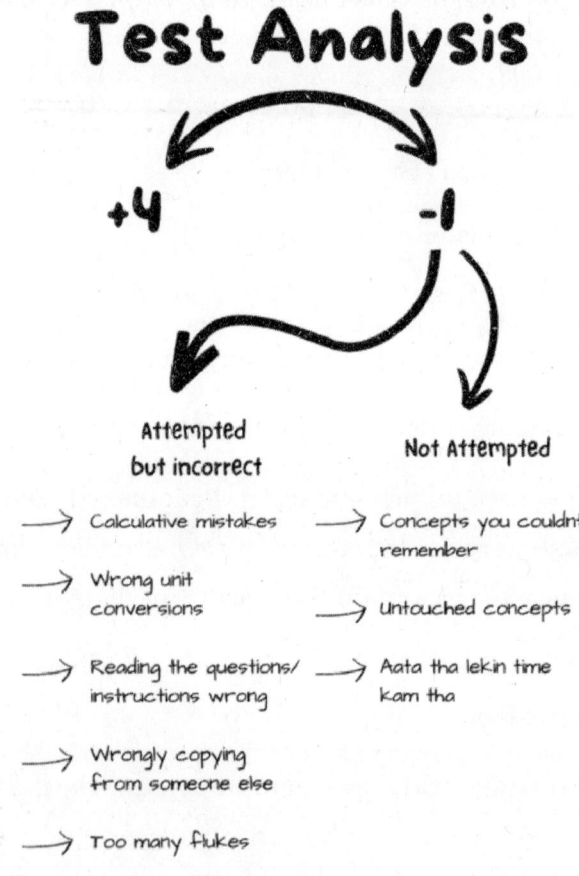

Do not, I repeat, do not make the mistake of ignoring this.

Note all the topics falling under Category 2... And before your next test, revise them all.

If you get more time in between, try to reattempt those questions too.

That's all about analysing a particular test.

Q2. Bhaiya tests/exams ko attempt karne ki best strategy kya hoti hai?

Sol. It depends on which exam you're appearing for.

But in general, I find this one method to be the best for most exams...

1. Read the instructions carefully
2. Now attempt the paper in 3 rounds:

In the first round, attempt all the easiest questions... This will build your confidence.

In the second round, attempt questions that are 1 level higher in toughness.

This will set the right tone for round 3...

And then in the final round, attempt all the remaining questions.

This includes questions that are:
- the toughest
- easy but calculative
- short but tricky

Q3. Kya tests me tukke marne sahi hai?

Sol. Dekho, it depends. Lemme discuss an interesting story with you.

Everyone (after exam) was gossiping and having lunch in mess when suddenly Ansh joined us. He was jumping and vibing to Justin Bieber's 'Baby' song.

"*Abey Ansh. Lekin tu toh sirf hindi gaane sunta tha. Tujhe kya ho gaya?*"...

I asked, confused to see Ansh happy while everyone else was sad for not giving their best.

"*Jaise yeh naach raha hai,*" said another friend, "*iska AIR 1 pakka.*"

"Arey AIR 1 thoda mushkil hai..." said Ansh, *"Lekin questions saare phodd ke aaya hu."*

"Saare ho gaye?", all of us were in shock.

"Haa matlab last ke 10 min mein jitne bache the unme tukka maar diya...

Khaali thodi na chodna hota hai paper, mujhe meri 10th ki teacher ne bataya tha," said Ansh, looking like he didn't give a single f**k.

We all smirked subtly.

"Abey chomu, instructions toh padh leta!" I said, *"Negative marking thi test mein."*

Ansh's score was the highest in class...

...but from behind.

He scored -51/360.

That too in the very first test of coaching.

Bhaiya, -51 kiske aate hai?

Unke jo competitive tests ko boards ki strategy se solve karte hai.

Do not, I repeat, do not fluke in sections with negative marking unless you're 100% sure of the answer.

Even a single -1 will throw you back by hundreds of ranks.

Here's what you should do — **Act smart!**

Fluke crazily in sections that don't have negative marking.

(10 mei se 1 toh sahi hoga...)

And if you're lucky then maybe 10/10 will be right!

Q4. Bhaiya tests ke baad kaafi low and unmotivated feel hota hai. Sab padhta hu, sab revise karta hu, class mein 100% focus bhi karta hu lekin phir bhi marks nahi aa rahe. Kya karu?

Sol. This is what I used to do while going through dark phases:

Talked to my parents, friends, and favourite teachers.

"Kuch nahi hota Shobhit. Tere kam marks aa rahe hai matlab tu at least try toh kar raha hai. Bas aise hi padhte reh, mehnat karte reh aur tujhe results pakka dikhenge.

Aur kabhi bhi low feel ho toh hum hai baat karne ke liye," that's how they used to console me every time.

This will not make your marks jump to the top...

But this will, for sure, give you courage and self-esteem to stand up once again every time you fall.

And that sets you apart from the general crowd.

Q5. Bhaiyya kuch bacche tests me cheating karke acche batch me promote ho jaate hai usse humara to nuksaan ho raha hai na?

Sol. We had a guy named Shubham in our class. He was a below average student.

But guess what?

Within 6 months he had been promoted to the top batch of our coaching.

Lekin woh kaise bhaiya?

Shubham's benchmate was a topper... So in every test (whether a small class test or a main exam), Shubham would take help from his topper friend and cheat.

And that got him promoted to the top most batch that had the creamiest layer of Kota studying together.

Lekin kaha jaata hai na ki, **"Karma will eventually catch up with you."**

And within a week, Shubham realised he didn't fit in that batch properly...

And that everyone around him was 1000x more dedicated and intelligent.

By the time 11th got over, Shubham had realised JEE wasn't for him.

He got frustrated, stressed, and this impacted his preparation.

And unfortunately, he didn't get selected.

The point is...

Initially, this will fascinate you a lot.

Top batch, surrounded by toppers, everyone complimenting you.

But if you've faked it and it is not the real you then be prepared to face the reality.

Because in the end you'll not be able to cope-up with students around you and your dream will never be fulfilled.

Hall - B: 'Neend'

This section talks about your biggest enemy — **NEEND!**

These are the most common DMs students send me on my Insta:

- *"Bhaiyya roz sochta hu ki kal jaldi uhtunga/uthungi but kabhi ho hi nahi paata."*
- *"I'm preparing for 'X' exam and feel like I'm not doing much and unmotivated. I sleep for 7-8 hours and still feel overly sleepy every time I sit to study."*
- *"I feel sleepy all the time and can never focus properly. This makes me feel guilty and I end up wasting more hours procrastinating."*
- *"Padhne ka bahut mann karta hai lekin neend kabhi padhne hi nahi deti."*
- *"Bhaiya 1 ghante ki nap ka plan banata hu lekin kab 4-5 ghante nikal jaate hai pata hi nahi chalta"*

Exactly bhaiya, I feel like mera bhi neend pe bilkul control nahi hai.

Toh aao chalo, tumhari inn problems ka solution mai apne personal experience se deta hu.

Remember Krish?

Areeee, Krish from Chapter-3 (Raksha Bandhan)?

After that test where I first tried the *Anti Kumbhkaran Sleeping Technique* — " 2 hours of sleep. 4 hours of non-stop studying. Then repeat." — I fell deeply in love with it.

And then what... It became my habit.

And every test that followed, whether important or not, I was up with Krish, taking turns studying and sleeping.

Also we never quit and kept experimenting with crazy ideas...

...just to leave other students behind in this race and get maximum output in minimum time.

- waking up early
- studying late
- sleeping in parts
- applying Zandu balm
- eating only coffee and biscuits so we don't feel full
- placing our alarms far from us so we had to get out of bed to switch them off

Unfortunately, nothing worked...

And within weeks, we both saw our:

- routines getting f***ed
- concepts fading away
- health going down
- hunger getting messed up

Even though *Anti Kumbhkaran Sleeping Technique* worked well and got us good grades in tests for a short time, we realised one thing...

That it was not at all healthy for us.

At last, we came to a conclusion — **Either become a morning hen or a night owl!**

And another thing that separates a topper from an average student is how disciplined they are with their routines.

So, **Have A Routine!**

For all the morning hens in the house, this will be the most high-impact and productive schedule you can follow to ensure an A+ routine.

— Sleep at 10 pm to get up at 5 am.

(The morning sun's vibrant rays will set you up for an entire study day.)

And this is for all the night owls in the house...

— Sleep at 2 am (max) to wake up at 9 am.

(The glistening moon's silhouette will keep you energised for late night study sessions.)

Now, answering some of the most common questions students ask me regarding their 'Neend':

Q1. Bhaiya I want to study 10-12 hours a day but can't manage to reduce my sleep (7-8 hours). What should I do?

Sol. See, getting a good 6-8 hour sleep is as crucial as scoring good marks in mock tests.

If you think sacrificing 4 hours of sleep for studying extra will help you get top ranks, then you're wrong.

Even the sun takes complete rest for it to shower its sparkling rays over you again the next day.

10-12 ghante padhne ke liye neend par nahi distractions (khuli window) par compromise karna hoga.

Q2. Bhaiya will taking power naps in the afternoon affect my studies and routine?

Sol. Definitely. A 1000%... But in a positive way.

In fact, I personally am a big fan of afternoon power naps.

They are a great way to kidnap all your stress and tiredness and throw them away somewhere far.

Take a nap for 45-60 minutes everyday after lunch and you'll find yourself all fresh, rejuvenated, and full of deep intense motivation to study hard.

Q3. Bhaiya what should be my diet as a student whose aim is to get into his/her dream college and who feels sleepy all the time?

Sol. When I was at Kota preparing for IIT-JEE, I mostly had coffee and biscuits.

I had even slapped away every other food item...

No rice, chapati, sabzi, or anything.

Just coffee and biscuits.

This made me horrible...

I couldn't properly study... I couldn't properly focus.

My head spun most of the time and all I could ever think of was food and food and foooooooooood.

So, having proper balanced meals should be your top priority.

Include these items in your everyday meals:

- vegetables and fruits

- milk

- chicken/eggs/paneer

- nuts

Another toxic habit you should eliminate right now is eating heavy meals during lunch and dinner.

Your energy is limited. You have to make sure you spend it the right way on the right stuff.

Heavy meals drain you up and steal away your energy for digestion.

They make you instantly tired and sleepy ... and this is where most students lose their guard and fall asleep while studying.

Here's a list of some non-negotiables you need to follow to ensure you do not fall asleep (even after eating heavy):

1. Do not study in bed. Study on a chair and table.

2. Try out different study techniques. Pomodoro, Eisenhower Matrix, Eat That Frog, and many more.

3. Take frequent breaks and listen to a ton of music in those breaks. Try dancing as well. This will lighten your mood and charge you up for the next session.

4. Keep yourself hydrated. Water = ***AMRIT!***

And with this, you've successfully tackled all your **NEEND** related problems.

Hall - C: 'Stream Selection'

It was 3 in the morning. Everyone was snoring hard enough to wake up the neighbours around.

I was revising Inorganic Chemistry for the test ahead.

"Atomic radius increases down the group."

"Atomic radius increases down the group."

"Atomic radius increases down the group."

I was mugging up all the S-Block trends and properties when suddenly a sobbing voice caught my attention.

"uh huuh huuh", *"uh huuh huuh"* — the sound grew louder and louder...

And in a blink of an eye, the sobbing turned into a crazy burst of tears.

"Koi toh ro raha hai," I told my roommate, *"chal dekh ke aate hai."*

The sound came from the room opposite to ours ... and we moved quickly only to find out the door was open.

And as we opened it wide apart, both me and my roommate were dead-shocked to see Neeraj in that condition.

It was horrible... Horrible enough to make a fully grown man cry.

I still remember those disturbing visuals that kept me up all night, straight for a long week!

Lekin bhaiya, aisa kya hua?

Neeraj was standing upright, wearing his blue sparkling pyjamas and an oversized tee — staring himself in a mirror, his eyes all red and puffy and his cheeks wet with tears, looking depressed.

We ran towards him, and held him by his shoulder.

"Bhai Neeraj, tu theek hai na?" my roommate asked, *"Aise raat ke 3 baje roh kyu raha hai?"*

"Bhai sab khatam ho gaya," Neeraj opened up in a lifeless voice. *"Kuch samaj nahi aa raha kya karu..."*

"Lekin yeh toh bta ki hua kya?"

"Bhai sab sir ke upar se jaa raha hai mere. Har test mein mushkil se paas ho raha hu.

Quit karne ka mann kar raha hai. Ab aur nahi handle hota mujhse yeh sab bakwaas.

Maine pehle hi papa ko bola tha ki maths mein interest nahi hai, but unhone jabardasti Science Stream dilva di aur ab pachta raha hu."

"Neeraj tu ek baar papa se firse baat kar yaar. Aise rone se kuch nahi hone waala."

"Unhone itne paise kharche hai coaching pe.

Vapas chala gaya to saare rishtedar hasege mujhpar, kahenge 'Bas nikal gaya IIT ka bhoot sar se?' — Darr lagta hai bhai in taano se"

Neeraj was a strong person.

And after watching several Sandeep Maheshwari's motivational videos, he managed to get back on track...

And is doing great in life today.

But beware, future mein tumhari Neeraj jaisi condition ho sakti hai ... agar tum inn baato ka dhyaan nahi rakhoge toh.

And iss chapter mein mai tumhare 'Stream Selection' se related saare doubts solve karunga.

So, let's go!!!

3 out of 10 students in India are confused what stream to choose after 10th.

And even though today's generation is smart enough to make good decisions for themselves, there's still a big segment that ends up being a victim of this harsh society.

- beta science lelo, jobless nahi maroge

- bhai Riya bhi commerce le rahi hai, tu bhi lele

- arts lungi aur 2 saal chill karungi

Blindly following other people's advice will not only ruin your future career growth...

...but will also deprive you of your mental peace.

And trust me, you don't want to give your life's important (career-defining) exams with an unstable and chaotic mind.

Kyunki jab tumhe life mein wo sab nahi milta hai that you deserved... (just because you made a wrong decision by subconsciously getting society-influenced)... toh bahut regret hota hai!

Toh bhaiya, how do I make sure meri haalat Neeraj jaisi na hoye?

There are 2 ways to make sure you choose the right stream for yourself...

So you create your own unique path to success...

Way 1: Follow your mind

1. Goal: ✓	2. Goal: ✗	3. Goal: ✓	4. Goal: ✗
Stream: ✗	Stream: ✓	Stream: ✓	Stream: ✗

1. You're clear about your goals but not your stream.

2. You're clear about what stream to choose but not your goals.

3. You're clear about both your goals and your stream.

4. You're clear about absolutely nothing.

No matter how much confusion or clarity you have with your stream selection ... you'll fall into either 1 of these 4 cases.

Once you've figured out your column, I want you to do only one thing — **Research!**

Go out on the Internet and scrape everything down... Eat and digest whatever you find there... Then puke it all out and fill at least 10 pages worth of info you find.

Lekin bhaiya, yeh sab kyu?

The purpose of doing all this — **Writing things down brings clarity!**

Now you are clear about your goals, the career opportunities surrounding your goals, and the path you need to follow to bring them to reality.

So, reaching your goals will have multiple paths ... but you have to select only 1.

And walking the easiest path is determined by what stream you choose.

So, if you choose a stream based on society's lame and unimportant opinions... then you'll end up just like Neeraj — walking the most difficult path full of dangerous thorns and bushes.

But if you plan and write things down and then make a decision, then congrats, you just chose a path that has beautiful landscapes and waterfalls waiting for you to adore.

Take your time to **RESEARCH.**

Way 2: Follow your heart

Get ready for the most clichéd advice you'll ever hear in your student life...

I bet you'll even laugh after hearing it. But it works most of the time.

Sadly, there's something you need to be for this advice to work properly.

And only a few (very few) have this level of _____ in them...

Bhaiya ab kya fill in the blanks karna padega?

The answer is — **DARINGNESS!**

Have you watched TVF Pitcher Season 1?

There's an exceptionally beautiful and emotional scene in that series that features Naveen tossing a coin while making his life's hardest decision.

And no, he neither picks heads nor tails ... and yet gets an answer to his confusion.

Let's say you are unable to decide between science and arts.

On one hand physics, chemistry, and maths thrill you...

...while on the other, you want to crack UPSC and become an IAS officer.

And so you are madly confused what stream to pick.

Friends say to choose science ... and you all will then have fun for 2 years.

But at the same time, your crush picked arts and you're scared of not seeing her again.

Aisi situations mein tum kya karoge?

Mai batata hu — coin ko uchaloge!

The exact same way Naveen did...

Lekin bhaiya, bina heads or tails pick kiye answer kaise milega?

No, you don't have to pick one. In fact, you don't have to pick anything.

The moment you toss the coin and it's in the air...

...your heart will rain down a calling. It will support a side and tell you to go all-in in that.

It'll assure you of the future fruitfulness of the decision you make today.

And that is when you know what to choose and pursue — (all of this will happen while the coin glides the air).

Hall - D: 'Relationships'

"Pyaar Mohabbat sab dhoka hai bhai. IAS YAS bano aur desh ko sambhalo," said my buddy 5 minutes after his girlfriend texted him — 'I can't do this anymore!'

And even though our tummies started hurting as we laughed hilariously...

There was something deep in his words.

Kya pyaar mohabbat sach mein dhoka hai?

Aao pata lagaye...

Remember how Zeel had a girlfriend?

He's in IIT Kharagpur today.

And another friend of mine who too had a gf (even in college)...

...he couldn't clear the mark to sit for placements.

Toh bhaiya, relationships mein aana chahiye ya nahi?

I talked to multiple friends of mine who went through a ton of relationships during college. And they all had polar opposite opinions about it.

Some said a right partner will 10x your success...

...while others said it will ruin your mental health and throw you on a bed — making you wet those pillows all night.

And that made me confused...

This age you're in right now is very fragile.

Your thoughts change... Your hormones shoot to the sky... You crave people of opposite genders.

In short, you experience what the world calls — **'LOVE'**

"Zindagi mein har cheez ka ek sahi waqt hota hai."

My father always believed in this saying.

Everything has a right time ... but one has to be dead-smart enough to figure that out.

And aapka bhaiya baitha hua hai na yaha par aapki help karne ke liye.

So, don't worry ... cuz I've already picked up the right thing for you.

The only relationship you should have during your preparation years is with your _____.

Bhaiya, firse fill in the blanks?

Before I answer that, tell me 1 thing honestly...

What is more important to you right now? (focus on the 'right now' here)...

1. Top ranks in your school, district, state, or even in India or

2. Having a partner that shoots you *'good morning and mere baabu ne khaana khaya waale'* texts?

Of course bhaiya, pehla waala...

Pakka???

Google has proof of 1000s of your questions like — 'How do I get into a relationship?' and 'How not to be single in 2025'.

And now, even ChatGPT can vouch for it ... that how desperately you want one.

If you ask me, then honestly, the single best advice that I'll give you...

..that will save you countless hours, tons of money, and a sea full of emotional roller coaster rides is:

'BHAAD MEIN JAAYE PYAAR!'

90%+ school/college relationships are nothing but a waste of time.

And if you're thinking of getting into one then be ready for the worst to come.

Lekin bhaiya, wo kyu?

To achieve big in life, you must set your priorities straight...

And they should look something like this:

- career/education
- character/personality development
- health
- family
- friends

And then LOVE, if somehow you're left with a few extra hours and some energy in your day.

But most students make awful mistakes by trading their study hours with things like:

- Jumping off walls to bunk classes together
- Going to a cafe in the name of coaching
- Lying to their parents about their relationships
- Spending too much time and money on their partner

You have to decide:

Either use these career-building years hustling day and night, working smart towards your goals, and finally getting your dream college tag...

Or continue keeping your head on your partner's shoulder saying 'I Love You Sweetheart' a million times in a single day doing absolutely nothing productive.

You'll get a lot of time for all this *'baabu-shona' stuff*.

Focus on building yourself... Become more confident... Score top marks in your school and coaching... Improve your communication skills... Start hitting a gym... Make memories with your friends.

This is what you should be doing now...

Koi hatao yaar yeh pyaar ka punchnama idhar se.

There isn't much to say ... only that please don't end up being an **'aawara aahiq'** until you truly get what you want.

And yeah, **'MUMMY-PAPA'** — answer for that fill in the blank...

Hall - E: 'Physical and Mental Health'

Here's the single-most disturbing phrase that every Indian parent fears reading ... and is probably their biggest nightmare.

"13,000+ students in India committed suicide in 2021."

Bhaiya, aisi baatein karke darao mat...

Let's talk about this so-called social taboo.

And no matter how many newspaper articles, social media posts, or even tv news broadcasts cover this topic...

No parent, friend, or relative will talk about this with you.

Absolutely no one.

Like the parents of those unfortunate 13,000+ souls, even my parents almost came face-to-face with this nightmare once.

Just after Raksha Bandhan had gotten over, I made some new terrifying habits:

- The Anti Kumbhkaran Sleeping Technique
- The coffee-biscuit diet
- No sports. No exercising. No social gatherings
- Studying 10+ hours everyday
- Believing every activity other than studying is a waste of time

And on top of that, I was kind of a 'kanjoos Insaan' — ate only cheap junk to save money.

And one day, that *horrifying nightmare* came knocking on my parents' door.

And after that incident, my dad made sure I ate healthy food only, 3 times a day, and on time.

He also tied up with a local fruit juice vendor and strictly told him to deliver me fresh fruit juice at my doorstep every evening.

He even asked Nimit, my younger brother living with me in Kota, to keep a check on my eating habits...

... and whether I wasn't falling back to my old ways of sacrificing my health for studying harder and saving more money.

Lekin bhaiya, aisa hua kya ki aapke papa itne strict ho gaye?

Mai BEHOSH ho gaya tha!

Hein bhaiya, lekin wo kaise?

Unlike every Sunday, that particular Sunday wasn't a normal one.

And it had been only a month since my 12th started.

I had been dedicatedly studying for 30 days straight on a diet full of Parle-Gs and Nescafe coffee (because of the intense motivation you have after starting a new class).

And so, after revising for 12 hours on Saturday ... I went for a 4 hour sleep.

And the moment I woke up, I felt something was not right with my body.

It was 6 in the morning when I gathered all my courage and ignored my headaches and went to the bathroom to splash some cold water on my face ... to alert me up.

I was feeling dizzy and could barely hold myself still. Even focusing on my reflection in the mirror felt hard.

And in a blink of an eye, as I twisted off my toothpaste's cap to brush my teeth, everything went pitch black ... like a dark room without a single light photon.

'DHADAAM' — came a sound that scared the s**t out of my brother.

He jumped off the bed and ran towards the bathroom ... only to find me lying fainted on the ground, lifeless.

Somehow, Nimit managed to get me in bed and brought me back to life.

He immediately called papa and in a few hours I found myself calm and relaxed resting on my dad's laps.

And after giving my toxic habits a new makeover, not only I went from a '*maachis ki tilli*' to a fit and healthy chap ... but my coaching test marks increased too.

Oh my god bhaiya, mujhe nahi pata tha aap behosh bhi hue the.

Lekin bhaiya, I've a question...

Aap apni saari videos mein bol ke chale jaate ho:

- 3 baar revision bhi kar lo

- DPPs bhi kar lo

- modules bhi kar lo

- sample paper bhi kar lo

Toh self-study ke saath yeh sab karne mein 24 ghante bhi kam lagte hai...

Kaise focus karu apni health pe? Kaise nikalu time?

Remember in that 'Relationship Hall', how I told you to create a priority list and put health on top?

Do that!

Dosto se toh almost roz baat karte hoge ... toh baat karte hue walk karo.

Fast food ki jagah fruits khao.

Screen time ko 1 ghante ke liye limit karo.

Din ke 30 minutes kisi hobby (like football/cricket) ko diya karo ... just like Shailendra.

Then find your friends all amazed and shooting compliments like — '*Bass tere jaisa fit dikhna hai*' — at you.

Physical health toh theek hai bhaiya, but mental health ka kya?

Stress, anxiety, self-doubt, and pressure … inko kaise handle karu?

Whenever you feel like nothing's worth it … and want to quit and end it all at once…

Take a pause and follow these 3 steps that take < 60 seconds:

1. Sit straight,

2. Drink 2 sips of water, and

3. Go talk to your parents… Or someone you're really close to

That's it. That's the best advice you can get to fix your mental traumas.

And trust me, this is what I did 99% of the time in Kota.

(I was as close to quitting as a phone's battery is to dying when dad calls)

This is what toppers do because it works like a charm — EVERY. SINGLE. TIME.

Hall - F: '21 Days Challenge Scam'

Have you ever heard of the 21 days challenge?

Yes bhaiya, wohi na jismai koi habit build karne ke liye uss cheez ko 21 din tak lagataar karna hota hai?

Right, but only 50%.

Me, you, and almost everyone have tried this technique.

But we've been doing it wrong.

We do know how to tackle this challenge, but the puzzle lies in tackling it effectively to get better results ... and build better habits.

Each time we begin this challenge, our over-the-roof ego gets in between.

Let's say you decide to study non-stop for 3 hours every day. And you think of turning this actionable task into a long-term habit.

This is what 95%+ students end up doing:

They pick up their thick books, open trigonometry (for eg) and start killing its questions.

Initially, a high surge of confidence fuels a powerful desire to keep pushing ahead.

- Question 1: Killed

- Question 2: Killed

- Question 3: ?

And if by any chance they fail to consecutively solve 3-4 questions straight, *toh phir pucho hi mat — 21 days challenge ka ek hi ghante mei* **THE END**!

And to cope up with the guilt of failing that challenge, they end up wasting another 1-2 hours scrolling reels, stalking their crush's profile, or fantasizing their bright future.

'Ultimalety', relapsing into their guilt trip ... all over again.

And after this drama, they're left with only 1 thing...

REGRET!

Yes bhaiya, ek dum right. Kaafi regret hota hai jab to-do list puri tick nahi ho paati.

Lekin iss situation se bahar nikalne ke liye kare toh kare kya?

Actually the problem with you is you know what to do, just like you knew about the 21 days challenge, but you always choose the harder way.

Lemme tell you how...

In the above example, where most students gave up after 3 questions, the reason was they chose to solve the harder ones first.

And that brought their chances of completing the challenge to a horrifying 0.

Whenever you try to form a new habit, just remember to start with an easy task first, and only when you fully complete it, climb one step up.

Take going to a gym as a newbie as a reference for a sec.

Imagine what would happen if you pick up a 20kg dumbbell straight away without any prior gym experience?

No, you won't just fail to lift it, but will also embarrass yourself.

And hence, your intrinsic desire to transform your body and form a new gym habit would start to fade away.

That's why, start small, and once that small becomes easy, only then increase the task difficulty.

But it has to be gradual or you'll crumble back to ground zero.

This does 2 things:

1. Firstly, as you keep solving easy questions one after the another, you'll not even notice how fast 3 hours went by, and boom, day 1's target completed.

This will release the right hormones necessary for you to **press onward and complete the challenge.**

2. And by the time you Master and gain control over your negative thoughts that forced you to quit this challenge, 21 days would be over.

And congrats, **you have added a new habit to your inventory.**

And trust me, most students are lazy and will fail to even reach day 2. That means, **you just overtook your competition.**

Well actually, not yet.

There're still a few things left you need to know to actually overtake your competition and secure top ranks in your exams.

Let's discuss them in the last hall.

Hall - G: 'Busting Out Some Weirdly Common Myths'

I once asked a topper...

What does it take to have your photos on newspapers and posters with taglines — 'CBSE board topper (99.9%)' — spread all over in your city?

The reply was something I wasn't expecting.

"*Bas iss ek cheez ko dhyaan se samaj lo and easily 1 month mein ache marks aa jayenge,*" said the topper.

"Topper *hona* is not only about:

- completing the entire syllabus
- studying 10+ hours every day
- revising 3 times before exams
- solving DPPs, modules, and sample papers

It's also about this one underrated thing most students ignore... that costs them their clarity and focus," he continued.

"*Aur woh kya hai,*" I asked, boiling with curiosity.

"Ignoring all crap and focusing only on things that matter," he replied.

And after our convo ended, I understood what he exactly meant...

Most students with big dreams and ambitions same as yours either get gaslighted or waste too much time on myths this foolish society spreads.

And if you think you're smart and don't want average kids to score more than you...

...then it's time we burst out some weird myths together, shall we?

Myth 1: Ache marks laane ke liye 16-16 ghante padhna hota hai!

Sol. Depends on the type of learner you are...

- one who studies only before exams or
- the one who follows a daily routine

If you fall under the 1st category then even 10-12 hours a day are less...

But if you study like Shailendra (2-3 hours of non-stop focus), then 2 such daily sessions are more than enough to score good marks.

Myth 2: Board marks don't matter!

Sol. Half Knowledge !

Also, not the best thing to think about right now...

If you aspire to study in one of the top prestigious institutes of this world (any Masters), then they surely do.

Ok tell me...

Would you buy a smartphone built by highly qualified IIT engineers or someone who learned only from YouTube tutorials?

I guess you have your answer...

But if you have an inclination towards newly discovered domains like entrepreneurship or content creation, then they don't.

Mujhe hi dekh lo. YouTube ki journey mein meri BTech degree ka 0% yogdaan hai...

But this doesn't mean you'll stop studying...

Build a good skill stack

Aur abhi yeh sab apne dimaag mein mat ghusne do. Padhai karo padhai!

Myth 3: Coaching ke bina selection impossible hai!

Sol. Ask yourself this 1 question...

'Why do students join coaching classes?'

To get lectures and questions for practice?

You can easily get those without any coaching too. Youtube and Google have all these for free.

So, why do students spend lakhs in coaching classes then?

The topper friend mentioned these 3 crucial constituent elements that are the building blocks for good grades:

- Focus and Concentration
- Consistency

And...

And kya bhaiya?

- And 1:1 live interaction with teachers

Coaching helps you keep track of your daily progress and constantly reminds you of *'Duniya kaha chal rahi hai aur tum kaha chal rahe ho...'*

In short, only coaching gives you that *live interaction with teachers* ... which is impossible to find anywhere else.

Myth 4: Toppers hamesha Time Table follow karte hai!

Sol. This is one of Internet's hottest and most-loved time tables of all time...

6 am → *Wake up*

6 - 6:15 → *Brush*

6:15 - 6:30 → *Fresh up*
6:30 - 6:45 → *Nahana*
6:45 - 7:00 → *Breakfast*
7:00 - 7:15 → *Getting ready*
7:15 - 7:30 → *Packing bag*
7:30 onwards school…

Now, take a piece of paper and copy this exactly on it… Word to word.

And then, tear the page into two.

Lekin bhaiya, abhi toh aap bol rahe the yeh best time table hai…

…aur ab aap isko faadne ki baat kar rahe ho.

This time table is way worse than Urfi Javed's dressing sense.

Here's why…

What if it took 15 minutes extra while bathing?

What if it took 20 minutes extra to finish your breakfast?

What if you woke up at 6:30 instead?

Saare time table ki 'mother-sister ek ho jaayegi'.

That topper friend followed no time table.

"Toppers time table banate hi nahi hai," he said.

"Toh tum sab kuch manage kaise karte ho?" I asked, gazing at him with a puzzled look.

"Task lists bana kar…" he replied.

"Task lists banao, prioritical order mein sab tasks ko arrange karo…

And ek-ek karke sabko khatam karo. That simple!"

Myth 5: Bhaiya how bad is social media for me?

Sol: As bad as RCB's luck in IPL…

Epilogue

'Barbaad Hona' is an accident. *'Barbaad Rehna'* is a choice.

This is not a *'hey look I finished another book'* book.

Instead...

This is a *'hey look this book taught me a few extra things that I'll definitely try'* book.

And if you think only passively reading and completing it will help you get ahead...

Then, you're mistaken.

With all the info available to you on the Internet, in this book, and in my videos ... and yet if you act lazy in putting in the work I asked you to...

Toh phir tumhari BARBAADI hone se koi nahi rok sakta!

Ask yourself, do you really want that?

About The Team

"Yaar Shaleen, teri help chahiye. Ek book likhni hai."

"Done bhaiya. Ho jaayega. Mai google meet ka link bhejta hu, udhar discuss karte hai."

I messaged this to Shaleen Gupta on 15th Feb, 2025.

And then, the two of us worked closely together on this project.

- Several late nights
- Countless early mornings
- Endless moments of '*aur nahi hota ab mujhse*'
- Infinite ups and downs

But this roller coaster journey never felt like a pain in my a**.

He made sure the book always felt relevant and that it fulfilled its core duty of helping you!

"Bhaiya." Shaleen phoned. *"Wajahat ko message karu? Uss jaise doodles aur koi nahi bna payega."*

"Haa bhai, kardo."

Wajahat and his brother Amaan's artistic talent deserves more than just an applause.

And how can I forget my dear brother, Nimit Nirwan, who fine-tuned every little detail that made this book more interesting than a comic.

Love you guys. Thank you for making this a reality. I couldn't have pulled this off alone without you four by my side.

Ruko Zara, Sabar Karo!

Bahut ho gayi padhai ki baatein aur gyaan baantna... Ab thodi masti karte hai.

Lemme tell you a funny story from my 1st year of college when a sadist friend of mine ended up tasting his own medicine.

After months of sacrificing my sleep and studies, I managed to gain 10k subs on YouTube.

"Hamara Shobhit bhai to ab famous ho gaya!" My classmates kept chanting this the whole day.

We were in the computer lab writing code when this sadist friend gave me a creepy stare.

He gestured me to bring my ear closer to him and then vomited this...

"Kya bhai Shobhit," he said, *"tu toh raato raat famous ho gaya!"*

He was one of those people who loved satisfying their egos by trash-talking about others' achievements.

"Haa bhai bilkul." My best friend sitting beside me heard him and came up with the most savage reply ever – *"Ha bhai, bass woh raat 6 mahine lambi thi!"*

Aur phir kya, uss bechare ki shakal aise utri ki pucho hi mat!

The point is...

Even though I didn't make it to IIT, this separate journey forged me into the creator and entrepreneur I'm today.

Padhai-vadhai toh hoti rahegi, lekin asli maza hai kuch alag, apna kar dikhane mein.

Lekin bhaiya, alag matlab?

Aao btata hu...